J 597.89 DIC
Dickmann, Nancy.
A frog's life

DATE DUE

FEB 2 5 2013		
MAY 0 1 2013		
GAYLORD		PRINTED IN U.S.A.

Watch It Grow

A Frog's Life

Nancy Dickmann

Heinemann Library
Chicago, Illinois

www.heinemannraintree.com
Visit our website to find out
more information about
Heinemann-Raintree books.

To order:

☎ Phone 888-454-2279

 Visit www.heinemannraintree.com
to browse our catalog and order online.

© 2010 Heinemann Library
an imprint of Capstone Global Library, LLC
Chicago, Illinois

Edited by Rebecca Rissman, Nancy Dickmann, and Catherine Veitch
Designed by Joanna Hinton-Malivoire
Picture research by Mica Brancic
Production by Victoria Fitzgerald
Originated by Capstone Global Library Ltd
Printed and bound in the United States of America by Worzalla

14 13 12 11 10
10 9 8 7 6 5 4 3 2 1

Library of Congress Cataloging-in-Publication Data
Dickmann, Nancy.
 A frog's life / Nancy Dickmann.
  p. cm. -- (Watch it grow)
 Includes bibliographical references and index.
 ISBN 978-1-4329-4140-6 (hc) -- ISBN 978-1-4329-4149-9 (pb) 1. Frogs--
Life cycles--Juvenile literature. I. Title.
 QL668.E2D53 2011
 597.8'9--dc22
                    2009049156

Acknowledgments
We would would like to thank the following for permission to reproduce
photographs: Getty Images p. **6** (© Dorling Kindersley/Neil Fletcher);
iStockphoto pp. **8** (© Robert Ellis), **9** (© Sven Peter), **14** (Tommounsey),
20 (© Alan Crawford), **21** (© Jerry Whaley), **22 top** (© Sven Peter);
Photolibrary pp. **4** (age fotostock/Caroline Commins), **10** (White/
© Rosemary Calvert), **11** (© Eric Anthony Johnson), **13** (Animals Animals/
© Zigmund Leszczynski), **15** (Animals Animals/© Zigmund Leszczynski),
17 (Oxford Scientific (OSF)/© Berndt Fischer), **18** (Oxford Scientific
(OSF)/© Paulo de Oliveira), **19** (Oxford Scientific (OSF)/© David Maitland),
22 right (White/© Rosemary Calvert), **22 bottom** (Animals Animals/
© Zigmund Leszczynski), **23 top** (White/© Rosemary Calvert); Shutterstock
pp. **5** (© Steve McWilliam), **7** (© Katharina Wittfeld), **12** (© Wolfgang
Staib), **16** (efiplus), **22 left** (efiplus), **23 middle** (2happy), **23 bottom**
(© Wolfgang Staib).

Front cover photograph (main) of a common frog reproduced with
permission of Shutterstock (© Steve McWilliam). Front cover photograph
(inset) of a close-up of frog spawn reproduced with permission of
iStockphoto (© Robert Ellis). Back cover photograph of a frog and frog
spawn reproduced with permission of iStockphoto (© Robert Ellis).

The publisher would like to thank Nancy Harris for her assistance in the
preparation of this book.

Every effort has been made to contact copyright holders of material
reproduced in this book. Any omissions will be rectified in subsequent
printings if notice is given to the publisher.

Contents

Life Cycles

All living things have a life cycle.

Frogs have a life cycle.

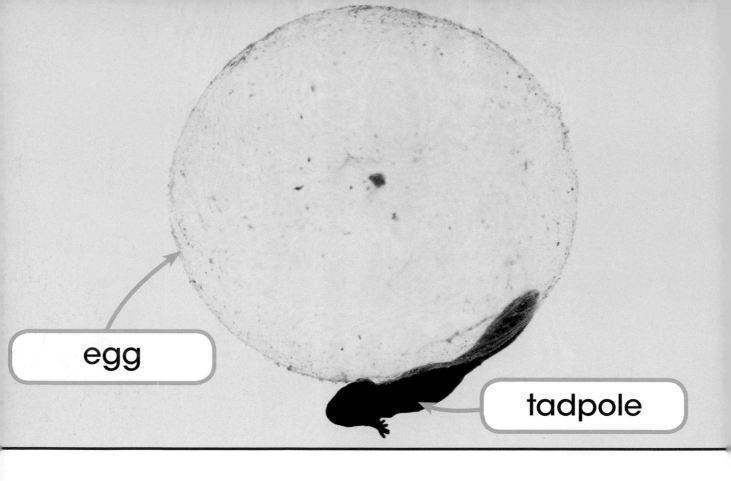

egg

tadpole

A tadpole hatches from an egg.

It grows into a frog.

eggs

A frog lays eggs.
Later it will die.

Eggs

spawn

A female frog lays eggs in a pond.
The eggs are called spawn.

Each egg has a tadpole inside.

Tadpoles

tadpole

A tadpole hatches from the egg.

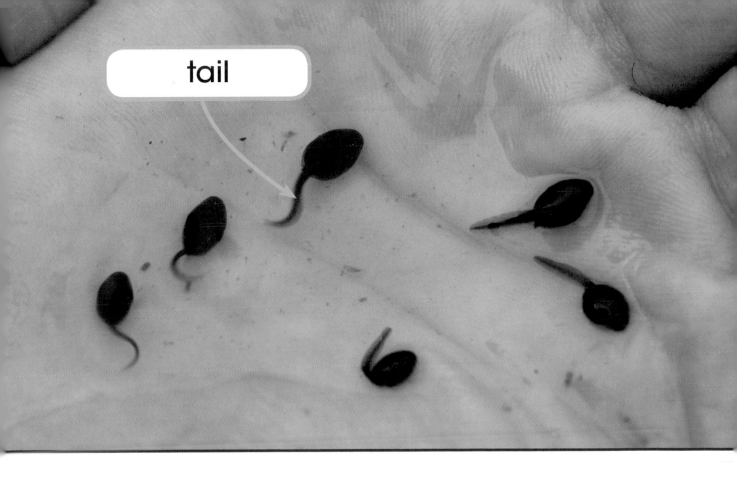

tail

A tadpole has a tail.

Growing and Changing

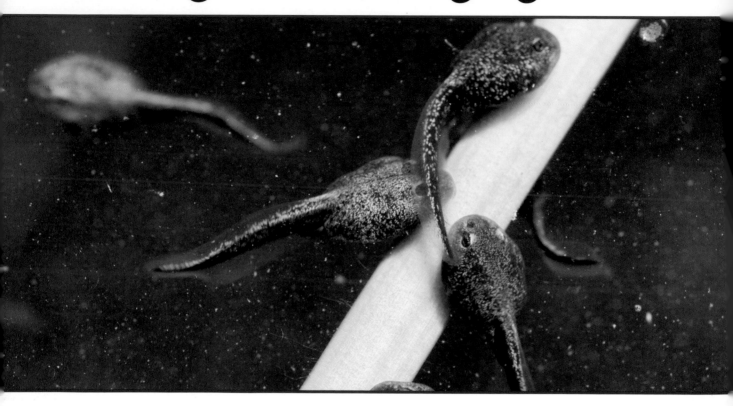

The tadpole lives in a pond.

The tadpole eats plants to grow.

13

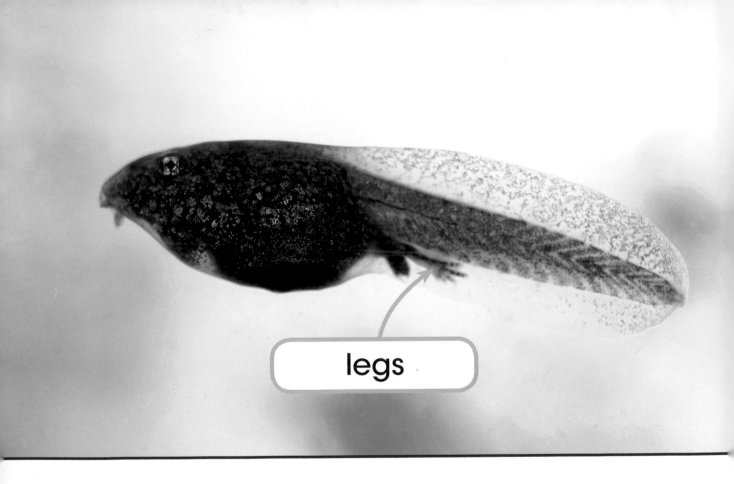

legs

Soon the tadpole starts to grow legs.

Soon the tadpole has four legs.

Becoming a Frog

The tadpole grows into a frog.

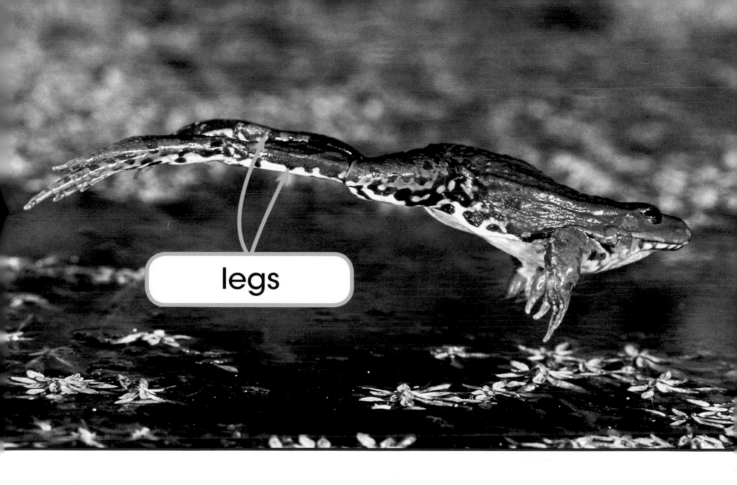

legs

When the frog is grown it uses its strong legs to jump.

tongue

The frog catches insects with
its tongue.

The frog also eats worms
and spiders.

eggs

A female frog lays eggs in a pond.

The life cycle starts again.

Life Cycle of a Frog

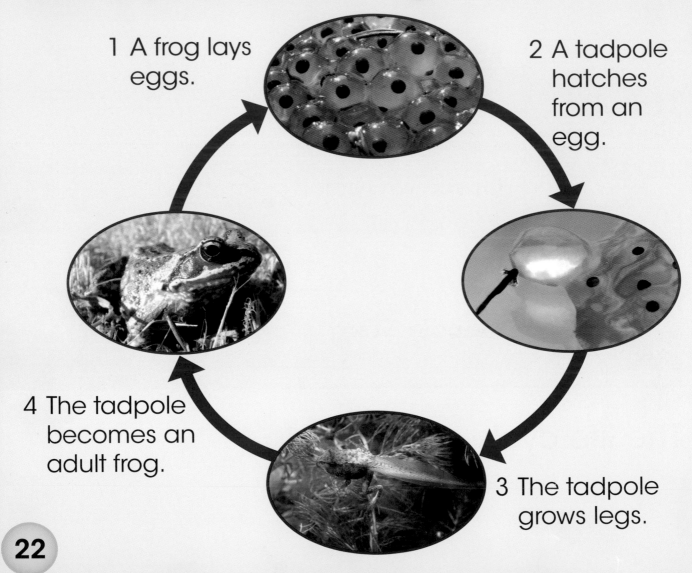

1 A frog lays eggs.

2 A tadpole hatches from an egg.

4 The tadpole becomes an adult frog.

3 The tadpole grows legs.

22

Picture Glossary

 **hatch** to be born from an egg

 **insect** very small creature with six legs

 **tadpole** young frog

Index

Notes to Parents and Teachers

Before reading

Ask the children if they know what a baby dog is called. Then see if they can name a baby cat, horse, cow, sheep, and pig. Do they know what a baby frog is called? Talk about how some animal babies look like small versions of the adults, and some animal babies look very different.

After reading

• In the spring, you could try hatching some tadpoles. Put a little frog spawn in a tank with the pondwater kept between 15°C (59°F) and 20°C (68°F). Add pondweed to the tank for the tadpoles to eat when they hatch. You can also feed them with lettuce leaves. Get the children to record any changes they see in the tadpoles each day. When the tadpoles grow legs, make sure there are stones in the tank that come above the water so the young frogs can climb up and breathe. Release the fully-grown frogs together near a clean pond.

• Get the children to dance the lifecycle of a frog. Start with them curled up tight, huddled up close together like frogspawn. Get them to "hatch" one by one and move around the room as if they are swimming like tadpoles. Finally tell them to hop around the room like frogs. You could play some music for them to dance to, for example Paul McCartney's "Frog Chorus".